BANJO *of* DESTINY

CARY FAGAN

*

PICTURES BY
Selçuk Demirel

GROUNDWOOD BOOKS • HOUSE OF ANANSI PRESS
TORONTO   BERKELEY

Groundwood Books / House of Anansi Press
110 Spadina Avenue, Suite 801, Toronto, Ontario M5V 2K4
or c/o Publishers Group West
1700 Fourth Street, Berkeley, CA 94710

We acknowledge for their financial support of our publishing program the Canada
Council for the Arts, the Government of Canada through the Canada Book Fund
(CBF) and the Ontario Arts Council.

 Canada Council **Conseil des Arts**
for the Arts **du Canada**

 ONTARIO ARTS COUNCIL
CONSEIL DES ARTS DE L'ONTARIO

Library and Archives Canada Cataloguing in Publication

Fagan, Cary

Banjo of destiny / Cary Fagan ; illustrated by Selçuk Demirel.

ISBN 978-1-55498-085-7 (bound).--ISBN 978-1-55498-086-4 (pbk.)

I. Demirel, Selçuk II. Title.

PS8561.A375B36 2011   jC813'.54   C2010-905898-4

Cover art by Selçuk Demirel
Design by Michael Solomon

Printed and bound in Canada

For Emilio and Yoyo
and Rachel and Sophie

1
The House Built from Floss

Jeremiah Birnbaum lived in a house that looked like a medieval castle. It was surrounded by a moat and ten acres of grounds. Swans and flamingos floated serenely on the water in the moat.

Inside, the house was anything but

medieval. There were nine bathrooms, a games room with antique pinball machines, a fully equipped exercise room with an oval track, an indoor pool with a water slide and a hot tub. There was an art gallery with paintings from the sixteenth to the nineteenth centuries, a movie theater, a bowling alley. The floors were heated in the winter and cooled in the summer. Hidden sensors turned on the lights when someone entered a room.

Jeremiah's bedroom suite was on the third floor. It had a grand entertainment center, private bathroom with a lion's-foot bathtub and a separate marble shower stall with stereo speakers built in. There was a refrigerator stocked with drinks, and three walk-in closets (one for casual wear, one for formal attire, and one for toys). The desk where he did his homework would have suited the president of a bank.

From his private turret Jeremiah could

look down at the artificial waterfall that fed into the moat. His father had stocked the moat with trout. That way Jeremiah could enjoy the experience of fishing without the disappointment of not catching anything.

Jeremiah's house was built from floss — dental floss. His parents had made their fortune from a dental-floss dispenser that mounted on the bathroom wall. The dispenser used laser light rays and a miniature computer to measure a person's mouth and dispense the precise length of floss required. The deluxe model let a person choose a flavor, such as mint, raspberry, chocolate pecan, heavenly hash or banana smoothie.

It was something nobody knew they needed — until the television and billboard and internet advertisements told them they did.

And if you don't have one in your house yet, well, don't worry. You will soon.

Jeremiah had absolutely everything he

could want. He was a very lucky boy, as his parents reminded him every day.

"Not many kids have what you have, Jeremiah," his father would say. "The most advanced home computer available. A miniature electric Rolls-Royce that you can drive yourself. A tennis court with a robot opponent you can always beat. Do you know how lucky you are?"

"Yes, I do," Jeremiah said.

He meant it, too. What could a kid like Jeremiah have to complain about?

Absolutely nothing.

• • •

THIS WAS Jeremiah.

Curly red hair.

Freckles.

Pale skin that burned easily in the sun. (His mother made him wear sunscreen even in the winter.)

A slouch when he walked, even though his father told him to stand up straight. ("Remember, you're a *Birnbaum*.")

Hands that were always fiddling with restaurant menus, gum wrappers, wax from a dining-room candle.

A total lack of interest in the international dental-floss market.

Jeremiah understood that his parents wanted to give him everything because they themselves had once had nothing. His father, Albert, had worked as a store window cleaner, moving down the street with his long-handled squeegee and his bucket of soapy water. He began work early and he finished late, but he barely made enough to survive. At night, exhausted, he would look up at the cracked ceiling from the narrow bed in his rented room and dream about finding some way to make his life better.

Jeremiah's mother, Abigail, ran a hotdog cart. She didn't own the cart. She just worked for the man who did, Mr. Smerge. Mr. Smerge complained if her customers used up the condiments. "Too many pickles, too little profit!" he scolded.

At the end of each week, Albert would treat himself to a hotdog for dinner, loading it with pickles, onions, hot peppers and sauerkraut. He thought Abigail had a nice smile, but he was too shy to start up a conversation. Instead, he sat on a bench near the cart and ate his hotdog by himself.

One day Albert felt something caught between his teeth. He tried to work it out with his tongue and then, hoping nobody was watching, with his finger.

When he looked up, he saw the woman from the hotdog cart standing in front of him. She was holding out a little container of dental floss.

Albert said thank you and tore off a piece of floss.

"I've taken more than I need. What a waste, I'm so sorry," he said.

"That's all right, I do it all the time," said Abigail. "There ought to be a dispenser that gives you just the right amount, don't you think?"

And that's when Albert's eyes lit up.

Jeremiah had heard the story many times about how his parents had come up with the idea for their invention. How his parents' courtship was spent designing the dispenser. Abigail did the research on laser calculation, computer miniaturization, as well as the dispensing mechanics. Albert learned how to set up a manufacturing operation and distribution network.

Jeremiah understood that his parents had grown up with so little that they wanted only the best for him. But he didn't see why he had to be a "gentleman," as his father called it. Why he had to know how to shake hands and call people "Sir" and "Ma'am."

Why he had to wait until everyone else was seated before sitting down himself at the dining table.

"You have to know how to behave around rich and powerful people," his father said. "They expect a certain standard. Especially from children. Your mother and I never learned these things but you will. It's why we insist you take all those lessons. So you will be an accomplished and impressive young man."

Jeremiah certainly did have a busy after-school program. Every day at four o'clock one teacher or another rang the doorbell. For ballroom dancing. Etiquette. Watercolor painting. Golf. And, of course, piano.

Ballroom dancing made Jeremiah feel queasy. He had to wear a suit with tails and a bow tie. He had to dance around the empty ballroom with a woman old enough to be his grandmother.

"Head up! More manly! Feel the music!" she would snap at him.

Painting lessons were a little better, not that he was very good at it. He tried to copy a self-portrait by Rembrandt but it came out cross-eyed. His imitation of a landscape by Van Gogh looked like somebody's plate after a spaghetti dinner.

Etiquette was merely boring. He had to pretend to eat a meal without putting his elbows on the table and say, "These snails are delicious." He got double points off for yawning or rocking his chair back and forth. Playing golf, he broke three windows and clipped Wilson the gardener's ear. Wilson yelped and dropped the garden hose, spraying Jeremiah's father who was bending over to smell a flower.

Worst of all were the piano lessons. Because Jeremiah actually liked music. He listened to his satellite radio all the time — pop, jazz, rap, heavy metal, classic rock. But

Jeremiah's piano teacher and his parents insisted that he learn only classical music.

There was nothing wrong with classical music, except that it didn't interest Jeremiah. Maybe if his parents hadn't forced him to appreciate it, he would have liked it more. But instead of going out to play he would have to sit up straight and listen to Beethoven's Ninth Symphony while his mother exclaimed, "Do you hear it, Jeremiah? It's genius, genius!"

Naturally they insisted on piano lessons.

"What do well-bred people do in their spare time?" said his father. "They play classical music on the piano. Isn't that right, Abigail?"

"Absolutely," said his mother. "It's the sign of a good family. We can't wait to see you in the next school talent night. We're going to be so proud."

Jeremiah knew he was sunk. If he tried to argue, his father would remind him that he had once washed windows for a living. His mother would tell him again how she had once sold hotdogs.

"My life," Jeremiah Birnbaum said aloud as he lay on his bed and looked up at the copy of Michelangelo's Sistine Chapel on his ceiling, "is a very expensive nightmare."

2

O Beloved Fernwood!

EVERY MORNING the Birnbaum chauffeur, whose name was Monroe, drove the limousine up to the front of the house. Jeremiah would come down the grand staircase carrying his briefcase and wearing his school uniform — blazer, striped tie, gray pleated trousers and shiny black shoes. His parents would be waiting at the bottom to inspect him. They would make sure his tie was knotted properly, his shirt had no spots of juice on it, and his socks matched.

Monroe was supposed to hop out of the limousine and open the back door, but he knew Jeremiah hated that. So he let Jeremiah open the door himself. Unless, of course, his parents were watching.

"Where to, Jeremiah?" Monroe said one morning in October. He was supposed to call Jeremiah "Master Birnbaum," but he knew Jeremiah didn't like that, either.

"Anywhere," Jeremiah said. "São Paulo, Brazil."

"Tempting. How about school, instead?"

"Can't you be like a chauffeur in a movie? The cool kind who just does what the kid wants?"

"I'm sympathetic, Jeremiah, I really am.

But we don't have enough gas to get to São Paulo. And I do think you need at least a grade-school education."

The Fernwood Academy had been founded 103 years earlier by Lincoln Fernwood III, the richest man in town. It rose up on a hill above the town and looked like a gigantic haunted house with narrow spires and leaded windows and gargoyles.

Every morning at assembly the students sang the school anthem:

O beloved Fernwood
We pledge our hearts to thee!
Do teach us well, so that one day
We'll run this fair countree...

Parents paid outrageous fees to send their children to Fernwood. But there were also a small number of scholarships for bright students whose families could not afford the tuition. One of those students, Luella Marshall, was Jeremiah's best friend. His only friend, actually.

Jeremiah and Luella met in gym class while picking sides for a baseball game. Jeremiah was used to being picked somewhere near the end, if not last. But Luella, who was the captain of one team, picked him second. ("Because you looked so sorry for yourself," she told him later.) He was so surprised, that she had to point to him a second time.

Being chosen gave him an unusual spark of enthusiasm for the game, but even so he struck out three times, dropped a fly ball and missed two grounders.

"Sorry," he said to her when the game was over. "I guess I let you down."

"Nah, I like losing fourteen to nothing. But you can make up for it by buying me a root beer after school."

"I'd really like to but I've got a lesson. I

could give you the money and you could buy one yourself."

"Don't be a jerk. What kind of lesson?"

Jeremiah hesitated. "Ballroom dancing."

"Boy," Luella said, "you need me even worse than I thought."

Luella's own family lived in a perfectly nice if rather small house, and Luella took the Number 6 bus to school. Jeremiah had never taken a bus anywhere. He envied her independence.

When he took Luella to his house for the first time, she said, "Wow! Is that a real elevator? You're not just rich. You're *stinking* rich!"

The great thing about Luella was that she didn't care. Yes, when she came over she was happy to cannonball into the pool, or try to hit tennis balls over the net with her eyes closed, or throw balls down the private bowling alley while hopping on one foot. She even liked the swans in the moat.

Jeremiah was afraid of getting too close because they hissed at him, but Luella just hissed back, flapping her arms.

But she was just as happy to have Jeremiah come to her house, where they played Monopoly, read comic books, tried to stand on their heads, or walked to the corner store for a Popsicle.

Sometimes Jeremiah wished that he were more like Luella. He wished that he could do things without having to think about them for so long, weighing the pros and cons. That he didn't care what other people thought of him.

Luella wore one bright yellow and one striped sock to school because she felt like it. She stood up and told the math teacher, Mr. Mickelweiss, that putting questions on a test based on work they hadn't studied wasn't fair. She tobogganed backwards down the school hill, singing the Fernwood anthem in Pig Latin.

Jeremiah wished that he too could be brave and imaginative and even just a little bit wild.

. . .

AT FERNWOOD Academy, students were expected to be of sound mind and sound body. So once a season Jeremiah had to endure the school-wide cross-country run.

Being just outside the city limits, the academy was surrounded by fields of wheat, barley and corn. It was well into autumn, and the remaining stalks in the harvested fields had turned dry and brittle.

The students began in a crowded pack, but soon the faster runners pulled ahead. The slowest lagged behind, and the rest spread out somewhere in the middle.

Jeremiah and Luella always ran together. The truth, Jeremiah knew, was that Luella was a much faster runner than he was — one of the fastest in the school.

Jeremiah wasn't only slow. He also tired quickly. Learning the fox trot hadn't helped much with his stamina. But Luella stayed with him because she was his friend.

The two of them ran together, Jeremiah moaning about a stitch in his side, or his ankle hurting, or feeling like he was going to faint or die. Fortunately, Luella was a very patient friend.

Jeremiah gasped, "I can't make it. I think I'm going to barf."

"Oh, come on," Luella said, bouncing on her toes. "We're not even half way."

"I feel woozy. I might pass out any minute."

Luella rolled her eyes. "Okay, stop whining. I know a shortcut. Through that field. Then we can rest until the others catch up."

"You…saved…my…life…" Jeremiah wheezed.

The old farmhouse looked abandoned, the fence knocked down in several places and an upper window broken. Here and there weeds sprouted from the damp ground.

Jeremiah stepped in a muddy puddle, splashing his leg.

"Yuck. This mud smells awful. For all I know it's pig poo —"

Something made him hush up.

Music. It seemed to be coming from the front of the farmhouse.

It wasn't like anything Jeremiah had ever heard before, a captivating rhythm of plucked notes and sudden strums, melody and rhythm.

Jeremiah and Luella looked at one another and slowed to a walk. The music played on. It sounded weirdly old and jumpily alive at the same time. And as they came around the corner of the house, they heard singing.

Shady Grove, my little love, Shady Grove
*   I say,*
Shady Grove, my little love, I'm bound to
*   go away.*

Luella put her hand on Jeremiah's arm.

"Let's get out of here," she whispered. "We're trespassing. It might be an angry farmer with a shotgun."

"Since when were you ever afraid of anything? Besides, that doesn't sound like a shotgun."

It wasn't that Jeremiah felt brave. He just couldn't stop himself, for the music drew him on. It galloped through him like a heartbeat.

He kept walking toward the front of the house. Luella slowly followed.

As the music grew louder, he saw a man sitting on the porch's weathered steps.

He was an elderly black man, tall and slim, with a moustache. His steel-gray hair was trimmed short. He wore a white shirt with a pinstriped vest. His trousers were pulled up at the knees, showing his argyle socks and well-polished shoes. His suit jacket had been folded and laid neatly over the porch rail.

One shoe tapped lightly as he played on the instrument that rested on his right knee, the narrow neck stretched up into his left hand.

Jeremiah knew it was a banjo, even though he had only seen one in a movie or maybe in a cartoon. It was the most beautiful thing he had ever seen. It had an elegant neck with a design of vines and leaves on the fingerboard that shone as if it were made of pearls. It had a round body made of some dark, highly polished wood. Stretched over the round body was a kind of drumhead that was held tight with silver-colored clamps.

Jeremiah watched the man play. The

swift fingers of his left hand pressed the strings. His right did the complicated picking or strumming or whatever it was, using his fingers and his thumb.

Jeremiah felt something stronger than he'd ever felt in his life. He felt a desire — no, more than a desire, a *need* — to be able to make music like that.

The man looked up and half nodded at them. He sang another verse, his voice a little raspy. He played the melody one more time and finished with a final strum.

He looked at them again and smiled.

"Good day," he said.

"Hi. That was cool," Luella said.

"Well, thank you."

"We'd better get back to school. Come on, Jeremiah."

She yanked his hand, but Jeremiah didn't budge. He just stood there as if he was frozen, or paralyzed, or had been turned into a zombie.

"Do you live here?" he said at last.

"No, nobody does anymore. But I grew up here. We moved away when I was small. Haven't been around for years. But I had a business appointment in town and thought I'd pass by."

"I know that's a banjo," said Jeremiah, "but what kind of music were you playing?"

"I don't know if there's exactly a name for it. These days most people just call it 'old time.' It used to be played on the farms and in the countryside eighty years ago or more."

"Is it black people's music?"

"Jeremiah, you can't ask that!" Luella said.

"No, it's a good question," the man said. "In fact, the banjo is based on instruments played in Africa. The slaves first played them in America. Later the white people took them up, too. The music got all mixed together. By now I'd call it everybody's music."

The man stood up. He put the banjo into a case that Jeremiah hadn't noticed before. He was sorry to see it disappear.

"We're supposed to be running," Luella said. "We'd better get going."

"Nice to have met you," the man said. He picked up the banjo case and came down the porch stairs and went round the side of the house. Jeremiah heard a car start up. A few moments later he saw it moving along the dirt road. He watched as it got smaller.

"We're going to be last!" Luella said, starting to run.

Jeremiah reluctantly looked away from the car, and turned to follow her.

3
Not a Joke

"WHAT DID YOU SAY?" Jeremiah's mother's voice screeched as it rose.

They were sitting in the formal dining room. His father sat at one end of the long table and his mother sat at the other, with Jeremiah in the middle. He had trouble

CARY FAGAN

seeing either of his parents because of the two candelabras on the table blocking his view. Two servants dressed in medieval tunics and leggings stood with silver platters, ready to offer second helpings of the evening meal. There was duck à l'orange, potato croquettes and asparagus in cream sauce.

"I think," said Jeremiah's father, winking at his son, "that our Jeremiah is making a joke. The banjo! That's very good. Ha-ha! The next thing we know you'll be walking around in overalls and bare feet with straw stuck between your teeth. You'll be saying 'Howdy' and eating flapjacks."

Jeremiah looked down at the untouched food on his plate. This wasn't going to be easy.

"You always go on about how music is important, don't you? Well, I looked it up and you're absolutely right. It helps develop the brain. Music uses the left frontal cortex and the right cerebellum. And you know what? Musicians even have a more developed corpus callosum. Pretty impressive, huh?"

"Now, Jeremiah, there is music and there is *music*. Classical music is sophisticated. It's subtle and intellectual and challenging. You're already studying the piano. You've got a Hoosendorfer Deluxe Concert Grand to play on, the most expensive piano in the world. And even then we have to beg you to practice."

"Exactly!" cried Jeremiah. "Because I'm not interested in the piano. And I'm not interested in Beethoven or Mozart or Scarlatti, either. There's nothing wrong with classical music except that it's not for me. The music I heard...it was like... whirling in a field or jumping into a pond or...oh, I don't know. Please let me get a banjo. I've got more than enough money in my own bank account. In fact, I've got enough to buy a hundred banjos."

"Do you hear this, Albert?" said Jeremiah's mother. "Everything we've worked for. All those years of striving to make a better life. And our only son wants to throw it all away and…and play the banjo! It's just too much."

Jeremiah watched as his mother put her hand to her forehead and leaned back in her chair.

"Do you see how you've upset your mother?" said his father. "Jeremiah, I'm sorry. But we have to do what we think is best for you. We forbid you to buy a banjo. Now let that be the end of the discussion. And have some of this delicious duckling. It was imported from France and cost a small fortune."

• • •

BUT JEREMIAH didn't forget about the man playing the banjo. He couldn't forget.

He heard the rhythm of the music in the click of his bicycle wheels as he rode around the grounds. He caught the melody in the raindrops tapping the window of his room.

One night he dreamed that he was walking in a giant field of wheat. In the distance he could see a single tree with great overhanging branches. He began to walk toward it. As he got closer he saw banjos hanging from the tree like ripe fruit. But when he reached up, the tree's branches pulled away just as his fingers brushed them.

Not being allowed to buy a banjo didn't mean that Jeremiah couldn't *learn* about banjo music. He had his own internet music account, and his parents allowed him to buy and download whatever he wanted. He loaded his player with recordings by musicians with names like Clarence Ashley and Dink Roberts and Roscoe Holcomb, who were long dead. And with new musicians, too.

Each had his or her own peculiar style. Sometimes the banjo rang out like bells and sometimes it slurred like a blues guitar and sometimes it rattled like a drum full of gravel.

Jeremiah couldn't get enough of it. In the back of the limousine, lounging in the living room while his parents talked about how to reach the Asian dental-floss market, lying on his king-sized bed, his ears would be filled with the sound of banjo.

All this listening made Jeremiah happy, for he had found a sound that matched his own inner music. But it also filled him with a painful yearning. Listening wasn't enough. He would feel his own fingers moving in time, his left hand pretending to fret the fingerboard, his right plucking invisible strings.

"Enough with the air banjo," Luella said to him one day. "You are becoming a total bore." Jeremiah was lying on his back on the gravel of the tennis court, his hands moving while Luella sat beside him. "You don't want to watch a movie. You don't want to raft-surf in the pool or sneak up on the flamingos or do somersaults down the bowling alley. You don't want to play killer tennis."

"The last time we played killer tennis," said Jeremiah, "I threw the racket into my mother's eighteenth-century Italian birdbath."

Luella picked up a handful of gravel and slowly poured it onto Jeremiah's shirt.

"Hey!" He sat up.

"Oh, look. He's alive."

Jeremiah sighed. "I'm sorry. I know. But I can't help it."

"Well, we're just going to have to do something about this, aren't we?" said Luella. "It's going to be impossible to hang around with you until you learn to play the banjo. And you can't learn unless you have one."

"I already told you. My parents won't let me buy one."

"Then there's got to be some other solution. You know a lot about banjos already, right?"

"I guess."

"Didn't you tell me that in the old days a lot of poor people living in the country used to play them?"

"Sure."

"Well, if they were poor, how did they get banjos?"

"I don't know. They made them, I think."

"Now we're getting somewhere. Your parents didn't forbid you to *make* one, did they?"

"Well, no." Jeremiah frowned. "But how can I make one? I've never made anything in my life except that key rack in shop class last year. And you know how that came out. I don't have the slightest idea how to make a banjo. I don't have instructions. I can't use tools —"

"Stop right now, Jeremiah Birnbaum!" said Luella in her best schoolteacher voice. "All I hear is *I can't, I can't, I can't.* Do you think that's what the Wright brothers said before they built their airplane? Or what Louis Pasteur said before he invented moisturizing?"

"Pasteurizing."

"Whatever. The point is there's a first time for everything. Now are you just going to sit there? Or are you going to build yourself a stupid banjo?"

Jeremiah looked at Luella. His eyes grew wide.

"Come on!" he said.

For the first time ever, Luella had trouble keeping up with Jeremiah. He sprinted out of the tennis court and wound through the maze with its ten-foot-high hedges. He hurled himself under the waterfall and leapt over the miniature train that chugged through the tropical flower garden.

At last he skidded through the side door of the house and raced past the cook, who brandished a dripping spoon at him. He flew up the back staircase to the third floor. He ran down the hall, slid around the corner and threw himself into his enormous leather desk chair.

His computer flickered to life.

Jeremiah and Luella looked at the screen as he started to search the internet. They saw pictures of banjos — fancy banjos all carved and decorated with inlay, and banjos that were plain as could be. They found pictures of banjos played during the American Civil War, and banjos recently made in a factory.

And they found homemade banjos. Banjos made a hundred years ago and banjos made just yesterday.

"Look at that one," Jeremiah said. "It says the builder stretched the skin of a groundhog over the drum part. Am I going to have to hunt a large rodent and kill it?"

"If it was a contest between you and the groundhog, I'd bet on the groundhog," Luella said. "Let's keep looking. How come it has that peg or tuner or whatever part way down the neck?"

"That's the fifth string," Jeremiah said. "The drone string. You pluck it with your thumb. It's one of the things that makes the banjo unique."

"Wait," Luella said. "That one." She pointed to the screen.

The banjo that Luella pointed to was about the plainest there was. It had a very simple headstock. It had a flat neck without any frets — the thin metal strips where a person pressed his fingers to get the right note. But Jeremiah knew that banjos in the old days didn't have frets. Some of the players he listened to played without them. He liked the way they could slide their fingers to make the notes bend up or down.

The banjo Luella pointed at also had a body made out of a cookie tin.

A *cookie tin*? It was hard to believe. But a tin was round like the body of a banjo. Instead of a stretched skin, the bridge rested on the back of the tin.

It seemed a little weird, but at least he wouldn't have to kill a groundhog.

"I think—maybe—I could make a banjo like that," Jeremiah said.

4
What a Broken Chair Is Good For

JEREMIAH PRINTED off photos and plans from the internet. That was the first step. The next was to gather up the necessary materials.

Since his parents had forbidden him to buy a banjo, he didn't think he should buy any of the materials, either. So he had to find everything he needed. After all, wasn't that what a lot of banjo players did a hundred years ago?

Finding a metal cookie tin turned out to be easy. There was one in the pantry with only three cookies left in it. It was a pretty tin, decorated on the sides with old winter scenes of people skating on a pond and sledding on white hills.

After Jeremiah ate the cookies, he said to the cook, "I guess you don't need this old tin."

"What would I need it for? Keeping all my love letters? Now you skedaddle out of my kitchen." She waved a spatula at him, as if this time she might really tap him on the nose. Jeremiah tucked the cookie tin under his arm and ran up to his room.

He had his banjo pot!

Finding the wood for the instrument's neck wasn't quite so easy. It had to be at least twenty inches long. Since Jeremiah didn't know how to use any tools, the piece of wood had to be pretty close to the right size already. Straight and flat for the fingerboard. Narrow but not too narrow.

Jeremiah hunted around the four-car garage, but all he found was a pile of logs to feed the three fireplaces. Maybe a Tennessee woodsman could hack one into a banjo neck with his ax, but Jeremiah certainly couldn't.

He went down to the basement and found some lengths of cedar left over from the walls of the sauna. But cedar was too soft. He'd read on the internet that he needed a hardwood, or the neck would bend from the force of the string tension.

Jeremiah took walks along the road, hoping to find just the right piece of wood. He looked in trash cans and behind garages. But all he found was a cracked ping-pong paddle, a portable hair dryer with a missing cord, and a torn lamp shade.

Whatever a person might make out of those things, it wasn't a banjo.

One day after school he was crossing the grounds of the house. Feeling discouraged, his hands deep in the pockets of his uniform jacket, he came across the family gardener.

Wilson was tall, skinny and tanned from working outside. He carried a folded-up wooden lawn chair under his arm.

"Hey, Jeremiah, what's shaking?"

"Not much. What's with the chair?"

"Busted. The seat's ripped and one of the folding hinges rusted and broke. It served its masters well but now it has to go to the chair cemetery. That is, the garbage dump."

"Can I see it?"

Jeremiah took the chair from Wilson and looked it over. The legs on it were flat on the sides, looking kind of like giant Popsicle sticks. The back legs were longer.

Maybe long enough. Maybe wide enough, too.

"You look pretty deep in thought," said Wilson.

"Do you think that's a hardwood?" he asked.

"Must be, otherwise the chair wouldn't have been able to hold up your uncle Mel, if you know what I mean. Maybe maple."

"Then I think I have a way to recycle this chair. I think it still has some life in it."

"As the saying goes," Wilson said, "one man's junk is another man's gold."

• • •

THE GOAL OF Fernwood Academy was to encourage not only academic excellence but "well-rounded young men and women with practical skills for real life." Students took culinary arts in one semester and industrial design the next — what regular schools called cooking and shop.

Jeremiah had rather liked cooking. Mixing ingredients reminded him of making potions as a little kid, when the cook had allowed him to pour just about anything into a bowl, mush it about and put it in the oven. (He remembered insisting that Monroe sample his Tuna-Pea Soup-Chile Pepper-Chocolate Surprise.) In class he had made lopsided zucchini muffins and runny goat-cheese omelets.

Shop was a different matter. The blowtorches and electric sanders scared him. His last project, a wire key rack, had ended up looking like the skeleton of some small extinct animal.

Luella, on the hand, was good at shop. Her parents actually *used* her key rack.

"This year," said Ms. Threap, the shop teacher, "we're going to continue the rack theme. Only this time we're all going to make wine racks. Won't that be fun and useful? Won't your moms and dads be thrilled to have a place to store their chardonnays and pinot noirs?"

"My parents drink beer," whispered Luella.

"Less talk and more work," said Ms. Threap.

Jeremiah knew this was his chance. He was a little afraid of Ms. Threap, who barked like a drill sergeant and wore earrings that looked like miniature power saws. He looked back at Luella, who gave him an encouraging nod.

"Ms. Threap?"

"Yes, Larry?"

"Jeremiah."

"That's what I said. What can I do you for?"

"I was wondering if I could make something else for my project."

"Something else?" Ms. Threap put her

hands on her hips. "A wine rack not good enough for you, eh? You want to build maybe a houseboat? Or a jet engine?"

"I want to build a banjo."

"I'm sorry, Larry, but you'd better stick to the wine rack. Unless you'd like to try to make another key rack. Perhaps one that doesn't look like a rat trap."

"I really want to make a banjo," he said. "I've got the material. I've even got some plans and pictures."

"Plans? Now that's a horse of a different color. Let me see them."

Jeremiah hurried to pull the plans from his briefcase. Ms. Thread spread them out on a work table.

"Well, this doesn't look too hard," she said. "Not with a little assistance from yours truly."

"I'd appreciate all the help I can get," Jeremiah said.

Ms. Thread straightened up and smiled.

"You're on, Larry. You can build a banjo. Personally, I prefer the sound of the accordion. I just love my Friday night polka group. But that's another kettle of fish. Let's get you started."

The first step was to take some measurements. Jeremiah had managed to sneak the broken chair to school. With Ms. Threap's help, he saw that the leg was indeed long enough, and just wide enough, too. She showed him how to use a pencil and triangle to make a line and then use a saw to cut the leg from the rest of chair.

When it was free, he unclamped it from the vice and held it in his hands. It felt more like a fence post than a banjo neck, but it was a start.

The next task was harder. A banjo neck was narrower at the top. Ms. Threap showed him how to use a chisel and a wooden mallet to carefully chip away at the wood.

Jeremiah worked for the whole class and

then came back at the end of the day. When the hand holding the chisel slipped, his heart jumped. For a moment he thought that he had cracked the whole neck instead of just chipping off a bit.

Finally Mrs. Threap said she had to close up, and he brushed the wood chips from his clothes and ran to find Monroe waiting with the limousine.

He climbed into the passenger seat.

"I've been waiting almost an hour," Monroe said.

"I'm sorry. I had some extra work to do."

"It isn't me I'm worried about. You've missed your ballroom dancing lesson."

Jeremiah groaned. "Mom and Dad aren't going to be too happy."

"Not only that," said Monroe. "Today you were going to learn how to rumba."

5
Pedagogical Study Number Eight

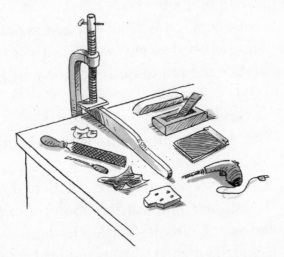

JEREMIAH'S PARENTS were indeed displeased to hear that he had missed ballroom dancing. But Jeremiah told them that he had been working on a particularly ambitious industrial design project that would require extra hours. He asked whether he could, just temporarily, of course, skip some of his after-school activities.

"Industrial design is a much more important subject than most people realize," Jeremiah said. "I mean, just think of the design work that went into the dental-floss dispenser."

"That's true," said his father. "What do you think, Abigail?"

His mother finished arranging some rare orchids in a vase. "I don't think missing a few classes would hurt. Except piano, of course."

"Thanks!" Jeremiah hugged them both.

"So what is this ambitious project you're building?" his father asked.

Jeremiah froze. Slowly he looked to the left and right and then over his parents' heads so he didn't have to look them in the eyes.

"I'd like to keep it a surprise. Would that be okay?"

"I know," his mother said. "It's for my birthday, isn't it? Oh, don't tell me. Do you think I'm going to be very surprised?"

Jeremiah nodded. "Pretty surprised."

• • •

PERHAPS JEREMIAH would have enjoyed the piano more if he had had a different teacher. But Jeremiah's parents insisted that he study with Maestro Boris, a retired concert pianist famous for screaming, ripping up sheet music and tossing it like confetti, strangling himself, thrashing his cane in the air, and otherwise striking terror in the hearts of his students.

When the Maestro swept in, Jeremiah was already seated at the Hoosendorfer Deluxe Concert Grand. His frightened reflection gazed back at him from its brilliant black surface.

Maestro Boris clapped his hands.

"Begin!" he commanded. "Pedagogical Study Number Eight. You have been practicing, yes? Let me hear."

The piece was from the Maestro's own book of music compositions. Jeremiah tried to steady his shaking hands.

He was not even halfway through when the Maestro began rapping his cane on the floor like a series of gunshots.

"No, no, no! A thousand times no! Do you think that is how Horowitz would have played it? Or Rubinstein? You sound as if you are wearing hockey gloves. You must be light, carefree, a butterfly flitting from branch to branch. And look how you slouch! Sit up, be proud. Now try again!"

Jeremiah started at the beginning, the Maestro banged his cane, and on it went.

When the half hour was over, the Maestro took his silk handkerchief from his pocket and wiped the sweat from his brow. Jeremiah's mother came into the room with an envelope of crisp bills, which was how the Maestro preferred to be paid.

"I am wasting my time," the Maestro said, peeking into the envelope and then tucking it inside his jacket. "Your son is without a shred of talent. He has no ear. I think maybe he even has no soul."

"Please, Maestro Boris, don't give up. The student talent night is almost here. We think it's just so very important for Jeremiah's self-esteem that he perform. He will try harder. Won't you, Jeremiah?"

Jeremiah thought *no.* Jeremiah said, "Yes."

"As you wish," the Maestro said with a sigh. "Perhaps next time you might have a glass of red wine waiting for me. Something French and very dry."

"Yes, of course," said Jeremiah's mother. "We're just so grateful for your efforts."

"Of course you are," said the Maestro, sweeping out of the house.

After the Maestro was gone, Jeremiah went down to the basement. His father had put a workshop next to the ultramodern furnace and air-conditioning system, so that Wilson could fix things. A long wooden workbench stood along the wall, with vices attached to it. On a pegboard hung hammers, chisels, saws, rasps.

Jeremiah had brought the length of wood home from school. Ms. Threap said the next stage was to round the back of the banjo neck so that his hand could wrap comfortably around it and slide up and down to play the fingerboard. Ms. Threap had told him how to put the wood in a vice and use a rasp, holding it in two hands and pushing it across to shave the wood.

Shaping the neck was tiring. The wood shavings tickled Jeremiah's nose and made him sneeze. But very slowly the back of the neck began to look rounded. When his arms ached too much to go on, he swept up the shavings and went upstairs. Then he took a long soak in the marble hot tub that was so big he could have shared it with a couple of hippos.

Afterwards, Jeremiah lay on his bed with his headphones on. He listened to Glen Smith playing "Sourwood Mountain" and Tommy Jarrell playing and singing "John Brown's Dream." Glen Smith had a quick, rough, plucky sound while Tommy Jarrell was precise and chiming.

They weren't trying to sound like anybody else, thought Jeremiah. They just sounded like themselves.

• • •

JEREMIAH COULDN'T work on his banjo for the next three days because his parents made him take his after-school lessons. And after dinner he had to practice piano for the talent night.

He did work on the banjo in shop class, though. Ms. Threap showed him how to smooth the rounded back of the neck with sandpaper.

"Getting there," Ms. Threap said. "But not smooth enough. You want it smooth as silk. You need to use at least two more grades of extra-fine sandpaper."

That evening, just as Jeremiah and his parents were finishing dinner, the doorbell rang. The maid let in Luella.

"How nice to see you, dear," said Jeremiah's mother. "You're just in time for dessert."

"I've already eaten, actually. Is that a sour cream caramel soufflé? Well, in that case..." She sat across from Jeremiah. "Really I just came by to see how Jeremiah is doing on his...um...project." She forked up some soufflé. "Yum," she murmured.

"Jeremiah's been very dedicated to his industrial design project," his father said.

"It's really very gratifying to see that he's inherited some of his mother's and my determination."

"Yes, very gratifying," said Luella, only it sounded like *wery grawifieen* due to a large mouthful of soufflé.

"And of course we can't wait to see it," said Jeremiah's mother.

Luella swallowed. "Oh, you'll be thrilled at what your little J.B. has got up to."

"Let's go downstairs," Jeremiah said firmly. "Now."

"Just let me finish this. It's fantastic. What is that wonderful flavor I detect, Mrs. B.? Ginger? No. Vanilla?"

Jeremiah's mother smiled. "Something French. It's called Cointreau."

"Well, it's sure yummy. Maybe I'll just have a little smidgen more…"

Luella took her time finishing. She slowly wiped her mouth on a napkin. Then she thanked his parents again.

At last they were excused and went down the hall to the back stairway to the basement.

"For a minute there," Jeremiah said, "I thought you were going to climb onto the table and lick the bowl."

They went into the workroom and Jeremiah turned on the light.

"I wish I'd thought of that."

The neck lay on the table.

"Wow," Luella said, running her hand over the wood. "It really looks like the neck of an instrument. It's nice and smooth, too. Is it done?"

"I've just got to use the last fine sandpaper."

"Man, I'd never have the patience."

"I want it to be a real instrument, as good as I can make it. And you know what? It's fun. At least some of the time."

Jeremiah picked up a fresh piece of sandpaper and went to work. The sandpaper made a soft *ssshhh* as it went over the wood.

While he put his energy into his arms, Luella talked. She was practicing a violin piece for the recital. She actually liked playing the violin. And she liked her violin teacher, Ms. Purcell, who always gave her a chocolate and told her she was doing very well although perhaps just a little more practicing would be helpful.

"Hey, I was thinking," she said. "How are you going to learn to play the banjo, anyway? I don't suppose your parents are going to let you take banjo lessons considering the fact they don't even know you're building one."

Jeremiah grinned. "I thought of that." He reached under the workbench and pulled out a DVD case. There was a picture on it of a man with a neatly trimmed red beard, a banjo in his hands.

"'Elements of Clawhammer Banjo,'"

Luella read aloud. "Well, I hope Red Beard is a good teacher."

"I've already watched it about a million times," Jeremiah said. "But practicing with a tennis racket isn't exactly satisfying."

"And watching you use sandpaper is about as interesting as, well, watching you use sandpaper. I'm going home to watch reruns of *Friends*. See you, Hayseed."

"Hayseed?"

"I think it suits you."

"Well, it doesn't. Never call me that at school."

"Don't worry, I'm not that mean. You don't have to see me out. I know the way, Hayseed."

• • •

WITH MS. THREAP watching over his shoulder, Jeremiah cut the headstock from a cross-piece of the folding chair. He drilled a hole for each of the tuners that would go in. Then he used a plane to shave down the top of the neck to a slanted angle and glue the headstock to it. To make sure the strings wouldn't pull the headstock right off, he put in a couple of screws.

"Not as elegant as a woodworker's joint, Larry," Ms. Threap said. "But it works."

Jeremiah would have worked on the banjo even more if he hadn't had to practice for talent night.

He was the seventeenth performer of the evening. Before him came six violin players (including Luella), two cellists, five pianists (three of whom also performed "Pedagogical Study Number Eight"), a trombone player, a jazz dancer, and a boy who recited the "To be or not to be" speech from *Hamlet*.

Jeremiah found himself daydreaming during the speech —

> *To be a banjo player or not to be, that is the question.*

*Whether 'tis nobler to suffer the slings
and arrows of disapproving parents
Or—*

And then suddenly his name was being called, and he found himself moving like a robot up the aisle and onto the stage.

He sat on the bench and looked at the keys that seemed to stretch away from him forever. He felt hot, unable to breathe. But he began to play.

As if they didn't belong to him, his hands moved too quickly, messed up and then stopped. He started again, this time too slowly so that he had to speed up. And then all of a sudden he started playing from the beginning again.

Jeremiah lurched from note to note, too soft in some parts and then almost slamming down his hands.

Kids in the audience giggled. Maestro Boris, who had come to hear his students perform, muttered darkly from the back.

His ears burning, Jeremiah hurried down the aisle, tripping on his shoelace.

"Hey, Birnbaum," hissed a voice from the aisle. It was an older boy named Damien Mills. Damien was a big, doughy boy who considered himself the funniest kid in school, even if nobody else did. "You got mixed up, Birnbaum. You must have thought it was lack-of-talent night."

Jeremiah practically dived back into his seat.

"Don't worry," his mother whispered, patting his hand. "We'll help you get over those nerves. I know just what to do. We'll hire a sports psychologist."

"A what?" said Jeremiah miserably.

"He works with famous athletes. To help them overcome their performance anxiety before a big game. And when the next talent night comes around at the end of the year — just wait and see!"

6
Putting It Together

"So tell me," said Dr. Barncastle. "Why do you think you performed so dismally at the talent night?"

Jeremiah sat on a sofa in the doctor's office. Across from the sofa was a large fish tank with gravel and waving plants and a shell that opened and closed, letting out bubbles. He watched the guppies and angel fish and kissing gouramis swimming round and round.

He had a lot of sympathy for those fish.

"Because I'm a lousy piano player?"

"Perhaps you can think of another reason."

"Because I don't want to play the piano?"

"Try again, Jeremiah."

Jeremiah tried not to sigh out loud. He looked at Dr. Barncastle, who was leaning back in his chair, a finger pressed to his high forehead. Dr. Barncastle looked as if he had the patience to wait forever if Jeremiah didn't come up with anything more interesting.

"Okay," Jeremiah said. "How about the piano reminds me of my mortality? You know, it's black and shiny — like a coffin! Every time I play I think of death. It freaks me out."

Dr. Barncastle smiled and nodded. "At last we're getting somewhere."

• • •

THE NECK OF the banjo needed to be extended with a "dowel stick" that would pierce through one side of the cookie tin and go out the other.

In shop, it was easy enough to cut another length of wood from the chair and glue it against the end of the neck. The tricky part was cutting the holes into the sides of the cookie tin for the dowel stick to slide through.

Jeremiah used a sharp X-acto knife. He had to be careful. The thin metal of the cookie tin wanted to bend or even collapse as he pressed on it. Also, he was a little afraid of the pointed knife. He was afraid he might slip and cut off his own finger. But Ms. Threap showed him how to hold the knife properly, and how to cut away from himself, and slowly he gained confidence.

But his progress was interrupted again by after-school lessons and three more sessions with Dr. Barncastle. Jeremiah felt crazy with impatience. At night he dreamed that Maestro Boris was riding a giant banjo across the black sky, cackling like a witch and waving a bottle of wine.

Finally Jeremiah finished cutting the metal. Holding his breath, he slipped the dowel stick through so that the two pieces of the instrument were together.

It looked like…a banjo.

Jeremiah felt his heart leap. But there was still more work to do. He had to attach the two parts together with screws. He had to make the nut, the bridge and the tailpiece.

The nut was a little bitty thing that went at the top of the neck. It had slots in it for the strings to go through so they would be spaced properly on the fingerboard. The strings would travel down the neck and over the bridge, which would sit on top of the tin.

The bridge, which he also made out of wood, was important. It sent the vibrations of the strings into the pot, where they would be amplified. The strings would be anchored at the very end of the instrument by the tailpiece, a little wooden triangle with five screws to hold the ends of the strings.

Even as Jeremiah worked on these pieces he wondered about the tuners. He needed four in the headstock and one for the banjo's fifth string on the side of the neck. They had to work properly in order to get the strings in tune.

And then, sitting in math class and thinking about his problem instead of concentrating on the equation on the board, he heard their teacher complaining.

"Does nobody know the answer?

Sometimes I think you've all got wind-up toys inside your head instead of brains."

Toy? The word triggered an old memory for Jeremiah. Somewhere inside his immense toy cupboard at home was a guitar. A toy guitar from when he was little, made of plastic. The neck was cracked and all the nylon strings snapped. He couldn't remember what the tuners looked like or whether they were real, but it was a chance.

Now he had to get through the entire day before he could find out.

When the limousine finally pulled up, Jeremiah threw open the door and got in.

"Home, Monroe!"

"Who do you think I am, the chauffeur?" Monroe said.

"Please be quick."

"Have something to work on? Something maybe to strum 'O Susannah' on?"

"How do you know?" Jeremiah asked.

"Let's see. Maybe it's the music you're

always listening to. Or that instructional DVD you carry around. Or that broken chair you smuggled into the car, or — "

"Okay, okay. Just don't tell my parents."

"I'm a chauffeur, not a snitch. Unless I catch you smoking. You aren't smoking, are you?"

"Of course not."

They reached the house. Jeremiah sprinted to the front door. He took the stairs two at a time all the way to the third floor. He flung himself into his room and threw open the cupboard doors. He proceeded to pull out railroad sets and microscopes, games and puzzles and model airplane kits.

Finally, at the very back, buried under a pile of stuffed animals, he found the guitar. He remembered now how it had got broken. A boy his parents had wanted him to play with ("he comes from an excellent family") had used it as a cricket bat.

It was smaller than he remembered, and

the neck wasn't just cracked but broken right off.

And the tuners? Yes, they had little metal gears and plastic ends. Yes, they turned. Yes, they were attached by tiny screws. They *were* real.

Jeremiah needed a tiny screwdriver to take out the screws. Fortunately he remembered that cook kept a little eyeglass repair kit on the counter by the spices. He took the screwdriver back to his room and carefully removed the screws.

At school, while Ms. Threap held the banjo. Jeremiah placed a tuner so that the little metal shaft went through the hole in the headstock.

It fit.

"Nice going, Larry." Jeremiah grinned happily. She handed him a screwdriver and he got to work.

An hour later his banjo was finished. He had to do only one thing.

Inside the pot, on the dowel stick that couldn't be seen except from the back, he wrote something using an indelible marker.

He wrote the word *Destiny*.

• • •

JEREMIAH LEANED forward to tap on Luella's shoulder.

"I finished it," he said.

Luella turned around in her seat. "What? Your project on Aztec human sacrifice?"

"No, the banjo."

"You're done? You're really done?"

"Who's talking?" asked the teacher, tapping her chalk on the board. "You again, Luella? That'll be an extra page of math homework for you."

"I'm sorry, Mr. Mickelweiss. I don't know what's come over me." Then to Jeremiah she whispered, "Meet me on the steps after school."

"Luella! That's two extra pages."

Luella sighed. "I'm doing so much extra work," she said, "that I should be able to graduate twice."

Jeremiah waited on the front steps of the school. He stamped his feet and watched his breath steam. The fall had turned cold, and the air smelled like snow.

At last Luella came bursting through the doors.

"I can't believe you're actually finished. How does it sound?"

"I don't know."

"What do you mean, you don't know?"

"It doesn't have any strings."

"Oh, come on, Jeremiah." Luella collapsed onto the steps. "No strings?"

Jeremiah sat down, too. "I tried this old fishing line but it broke. I read about a man who pulled wires out of a screen door to use as strings, but our house doesn't have any screen doors. I even tried dental floss —

mint, cranapple, double-waxed *and* triple-strength."

"You spend all this time building a banjo and now you're defeated because you don't have any strings. You're too much, Hayseed."

Just then Monroe pulled the limousine up the curving drive of the school. The long black car stopped, its engine purring.

"I have to go," Jeremiah said. "I'll call you later."

Jeremiah opened the door, only to find Luella sliding in after him.

"What are you doing?"

"None of your beeswax. Hi, Monroe," she said, shutting the door. "Would you mind making a small detour?" She leaned forward and whispered into the chauffeur's ear.

"I'd be delighted," Monroe said. He took a pair of sunglasses from his pocket and slipped them on. "What do you think of these? They make me look more like a real chauffeur."

"You *are* a real chauffeur," Jeremiah said.

The car began moving down the drive. Luella opened up her knapsack.

"You won't tell me where we're going?" Jeremiah said.

"Can you stop yakking so that I can do all this extra homework you made me get?"

Luella shushed him as she began working.

They passed fields and then houses and then the first shops of town. Monroe turned onto Stanley Street and pulled over when he reached Melrose Avenue. Then he parked in front of a store.

Melrose Music Shop.

"Luella, I can't *buy* strings…"

But she was already out the door.

It was an old shop, small, with some ukuleles and guitars on the walls, some student violins and a couple of electric keyboards. There were no banjos.

But Luella went up to the counter. The young guy behind it was stacking guitar picks one on top of another until they fell over. Then he started again.

Luella said, "Do you have any banjo strings?"

"What kind?"

"Kind? The most popular, I guess."

"None of them are popular. We probably don't even have any."

"Maybe you could look."

He rolled his eyes and then turned around and climbed onto a stepladder. He looked at one label after another and then reached to the back of the highest shelf. He blew the dust off a small box, making himself cough.

"You're in luck. There's one set. But it doesn't have a price on it. I can charge you five bucks."

Luella pulled a fistful of change from her pocket and poured it onto the counter. She counted it coin by coin.

"I've only got three dollars and sixty-five cents."

"Better than nothing," the young guy said, sweeping up the change.

Luella picked up the packet of strings and went out again, Jeremiah following.

"Luella, what are you doing?"

Luella stopped on the sidewalk. "Doing? I'm not doing anything. I really don't know why I bought these strings. I don't even play the banjo."

She took another step and tossed the packet into an open trash can. Then she turned in a huff and went to the car.

Jeremiah looked at the packet resting on a brown banana peel, a stained coffee lid and a container of ketchup-smothered fries. He hesitated a moment and then snatched it up by the corner and ran after her.

7
Bum-Diddy

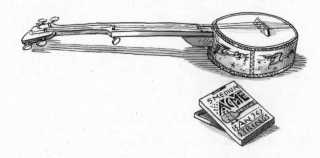

THE BANJO lay on Jeremiah's bed, strung up and ready to play. He thought it looked pretty good. It had a long, straight neck. The wooden bridge held the five taut strings over the cookie-tin pot.

Jeremiah had carefully turned the tuners

to get each string in tune. He had held the banjo in his lap and felt the smooth rounded back of the neck with his left hand. He had plucked each string with his finger, and they had rung out sounding like a real banjo, bright and tinny and clear.

Now all he had to do was learn how to play it.

He put his blanket and pillows against the door to muffle the sound so that his parents wouldn't hear. He had the DVD, "Elements of Clawhammer Banjo," in his computer.

He picked up the banjo, sat down in his desk chair, and pressed Play.

The young man with the trimmed red beard appeared. He had an easy smile and a jokey personality that made Jeremiah feel as if a giraffe could learn how to play the banjo.

But he didn't feel the same way after working for an hour on what the man called "the basic strum." This was how the right hand plucked the strings, and it required three movements in a rhythm known as "bum-diddy."

First Jeremiah had to pluck a single string with the back of a fingernail.

Then he had to strum the strings with his hand in a "claw" shape. Then he had to pluck the fifth string with his thumb. And he had to do it smoothly, over and over.

At the end of the hour, Jeremiah's head ached. The tips of his fingers hurt, and his back was sore. When he heard the maid ringing for dinner, he was only too glad to go down.

• • •

"So can you play it yet?" Luella plonked herself down at the lunch table across from him with her tray.

Jeremiah just looked at her.

"What's with the death stare? Don't tell

me. Let me guess. It's…ah…actually *hard*?"

"I kind of thought it would just come to me."

"Sure, because you're a once-in-a-generation prodigy. A born genius of the five-string banjo. It's a musical instrument, Jeremiah. You think only the piano is difficult?"

"I don't think I have the talent for it." He pushed away his plate of ravioli.

"If you're not going to eat that," she said, spearing one with her fork. "You know what, Jeremiah? I think you should quit. After all, you've been at it for…how long is it now? Oh, right, a whole day. Just because it's what you wanted to do more than anything else in the world shouldn't make a difference. Yeah, I say chuck it."

"That's pretty obvious psychology you're trying to use on me."

"For me to use psychology on you, you'd have to actually have a brain."

"Well, you'd find it hard, too."

"Yeah, but I don't want to play the banjo. You're not going to eat that chocolate pudding, either? No sense letting it go to waste. So, what exactly are you going to do?"

"Try again, I guess."

"Excellent. I knew you'd listen to your inner nerd."

"Sometimes I really hate you, Luella."

"Does that mean that the rest of the time you *love* me?" She fluttered her eyelashes at him. Then she said, "See you later," put her tray on her head, and balanced it there as she walked away.

• • •

THAT EVENING, Jeremiah practiced for another hour. And the next night and the next. And the one after that.

On Saturday his parents went out of

town to judge a tri-county speed-flossing contest. They asked Jeremiah if he wanted to go with them. But Jeremiah said that he still had to work on his school project, so they left him behind.

He put on the DVD again and then practiced the basic strum, doing what Red Beard had demonstrated. He groaned in frustration and put down the banjo. He went downstairs, raided the fridge for leftover grilled calamari, and watched a TV rerun about some kid called the Beaver.

But he couldn't stay away. He turned the TV off and marched back upstairs and grabbed the banjo. He placed the pot on his right knee, held the neck with his left hand, and strummed.

His strumming felt easier. His rhythm was more regular. It even sounded…okay.

Jeremiah strummed on and on. He sped up, messed up, started again.

He had it. He really had it! He stood up,

holding the banjo by the neck, and danced around.

"Yes, yes, yes! *Woohoo!*"

• • •

THE FIRST TUNE Jeremiah learned was called "Black-Eyed Suzie." It had a couple of neat slides in it, when he had to move a finger of his left hand along a string, making the note rise up.

Three days later he learned "Barlow Knife," and after that, "Salt River."

Because he didn't have frets, he made some small marks with a Sharpie pen on the side of the neck to help him know where to put the fingers of his left hand. He discovered that there were several ways to tune a banjo. It was often these tunings that gave the tunes their off-kilter, mournful sound — like the sad mewling of a lonely cat.

As playing became more natural, Jeremiah

was able to practice longer — up to two hours a day if his parents were out at the dispenser factory. Over the weeks he developed calluses on the fingers of his left hand. He learned how to do "hammer-ons," hitting the fretboard with a finger to sound a note, and "pull-offs," which were the opposite. Harder to learn were "double-thumbing" and "drop-thumbing," to play quicker notes and more complicated melodies.

He gradually picked up speed. Sometimes, when he was in a real groove, it felt as if he was galloping along.

After three months he knew he was still a beginner, but he began to think of himself as a banjo player. And the only one who knew was Luella.

"You're lucky that your parents forgot about the shop project," Luella said. "But at some point you're going to have to tell them."

"As long as that point isn't today," Jeremiah said.

8
Flower Power

Spring arrived. Jeremiah played his banjo every chance he could get. When he had learned everything on the DVD, he moved on to a book for intermediate clawhammer players. He practiced scales and arpeggios and exercises. He learned new tunes.

At first when he tried to sing as he played, his hands got all mixed up. But gradually he learned to do two things at once. He sang "Little Birdy" and "Cluck Old Hen." And the song he had first heard on that porch so long ago, "Shady Grove."

He didn't always practice. A lot of the time he played for fun. His room had a stairway up to a turret overlooking the vast back garden. Sometimes in the evening, when his parents were at a dentists' convention or a golf club dinner, he would sit out there and play.

The banjo sounded right outside, with the chirping of birds and the splash from the waterfall below. He could play for a good hour before running out of tunes he knew.

One day in May, Luella leaned back in math class and said to Jeremiah, "I made you something."

"What is it?"

"You'll find out if you invite me for dinner."

"I'll ask my parents."

"Your parents *adore* me."

"Okay, fine. Come tonight."

"Well, if you insist."

In the limousine home, Luella wouldn't tell him what she had made. Nor while they were doing their homework together. At dinner she acted the perfect guest. She always said please and thank you. She even encouraged Jeremiah's parents with their idea to have a miniature yacht built for the moat.

Then, in the middle of dessert (cherry meringue surprise), she turned to Jeremiah.

"I'm so excited about the spring talent night," she said in her best goody-goody voice. "I can't decide which violin piece to play. What about you, Jeremiah? Are you playing piano again?"

"I haven't really —"

"Of course he is," said his father. "Maestro Boris thinks Jeremiah has really improved."

"He said I wasn't as terrible as before," Jeremiah said.

"Well, it's the same thing," said his mother. "I think you should play something by Bach. It's good to be ambitious. Isn't it, Luella?"

"Oh, absolutely, Mrs. B. And I'm sure Jeremiah's up to it. He's so modest."

Up in his room, Jeremiah said to Luella, "I could have murdered you for that. I've been trying to find a way to get out of talent night. Now they'll never let me skip it. Thanks a bunch."

"Do you want to see my present or not?"

"Not if it's got anything to do with talent night."

"Well, it doesn't." She opened her knapsack and pulled out a folded wad of heavy material.

It looked like a quilt. Except when Luella unfolded it, Jeremiah saw it had two cloth straps and a zipper running up the side.

"What is it, a giant diaper bag?"

"You can't tell? Geez. It's a bag to carry that tin can in."

"A gig bag! Cool. Let me try it."

Jeremiah unzipped the side and slipped his banjo into it. He zipped it up again and put a strap over each shoulder. Then he paced around his room with the banjo on his back.

"Hey, this is great. I can take it around with me. I can go and play in the park. I can take it to a jam session, if I ever find one."

"You want to make jam?"

"No, a jam session. Where musicians come together to play." He slipped the bag off his shoulders and held it in front of him. "Do you think these flowers on it look a little silly?"

"Haven't you heard of Flower Power? Anyway, I made it from my grandmother's old dressing gown. It was the only material I had. You should bring Destiny to school tomorrow."

Jeremiah put it back on his shoulders.

"Maybe I will," he said.

• • •

JEREMIAH HAD TO slip out of the house without his parents seeing the Flower Power banjo bag. He kept it against his side as he passed the dining room. Fortunately his father had the latest copy of *Annals of Dental Floss* in front of his face. He was reading aloud the latest figures from Scandinavia.

"Those Scandinavians have healthy gums," said Jeremiah's mother.

Jeremiah threw himself into the back of the limousine, slamming the door shut behind him. Monroe glanced into his rearview mirror as he pulled out of the drive.

"Luella did a fine job with that bag," Monroe said.

"I must be crazy taking it to school," Jeremiah said. "It's like committing social suicide."

"That reminds me," said Monroe, "of when I was the first boy to wear bellbottoms to school. Bright red with peace symbols all over them."

"Did the other kids make fun of you?"

"Worse. But then Mary-Beth Matheson came up and told me that she liked them. Made it all worth it."

"Well, there's no Mary-Beth Matheson in my life."

"Maybe you just haven't met her yet."

The limousine pulled up in front of the school just as the bell rang. Jeremiah sprang out, his briefcase in one hand and his banjo bag on his shoulder.

No sooner had he begun walking up the stairs when someone called out, "What's in that giant purse of yours, Birnbaum?" It was Damien Mills. "Let me guess. Your portable crib?"

Luella came up to him as he was putting the bag inside his locker.

"Gee, thanks for the idea of bringing the banjo to school," he said. "I'm Mr. Popularity."

"That's because they don't know what's in it," Luella said. "Just wait till lunch time. You can play outside."

"No way. I'm not completely insane."

"Come on. You want people to hear. Otherwise you wouldn't have brought it."

Jeremiah sighed. The truth was he did — kind of — want people to see his homemade banjo and hear him play.

"Okay," he said. "But I'll probably have to transfer to a different school afterwards. Maybe even a different planet."

Usually lunch time seemed to take forever to arrive, but today it came all too quickly. Luella and Jeremiah ate in the cafeteria. Then they went to get the Flower Power bag out of his locker.

Spring was ready to become summer and the trees were green and full. Flowers filled the air with their scents. Bees hummed as they winged by. Students in their uniforms sat on the lush grass. Some threw Frisbees on the lawn.

Jeremiah and Luella walked to a maple tree and sat on the ground. Jeremiah undid the zipper on the side of the bag and pulled out the banjo. He started to tune it.

"What the heck is that? A garbage can on a stick?"

Of course Damien Mills would have to show up.

A few people on the lawn laughed.

Jeremiah started to put the banjo back in the bag.

Luella smacked Jeremiah on the arm to make him stop.

"Don't you have anything better to do, Damien? Like set the science lab on fire again?"

"That was an accident." He turned to Jeremiah. "So what is that anyway?"

"A banjo," Jeremiah said quietly.

"Can you play it?"

"A little."

Luella looked at him. Jeremiah put the pot on his right knee and positioned his hands. He started to play "Barlow Knife." He made a couple of mistakes, but then he got into the rhythm of it.

People stopped talking to listen. He played it a few times and finished with a brush of his fingers across the strings.

There was a scattering of applause. Someone even hooted.

Jeremiah didn't dare look up. Instead he started to play "Shady Grove." He didn't have the nerve to sing the words. Out of the corner of his eye he could see three or four kids move closer.

"Cool." He looked up and saw Damien Mills. "Can you play something else?"

Jeremiah played "Little Gray Mule." It was a fast tune with a lot of double-thumbing. He played it a little *too* fast and it almost got away from him, but he got to the end.

The bell rang. His heart now racing, Jeremiah put the banjo back in the bag. For the first time he felt like a real musician.

Luella nudged him with her elbow as she stood up.

"Nice going, Hayseed."

"Hayseed! " cried Damien. "That's a good name for you. Hayseed Birnbaum. See you at the square dance, Hayseed."

A couple of kids laughed. He heard somebody repeat the name Hayseed.

Jeremiah just shook his head. He knew the moment had been too good to be true.

9

Something by Bach

"WHAT ARE YOU having for lunch, Hayseed? Grits?"

"Hey, Hayseed, it's time to milk the cows!"

"Hayseed, your grandpa just fell out of the rocking chair and lost his false teeth!"

Jeremiah didn't know what grits were.

But it didn't matter. Even some of the kids who had liked his playing were calling him Hayseed. Jeremiah just kept his head down and didn't answer. But if Luella was around it was a different story.

"How would you like me to knock the hay out of *you*?"

"Just what I need," Jeremiah said to her at their lockers. "My own personal defender. Why don't you put on a mask and cape?"

"I know it's my fault," Luella said. "But you know what? It's not a bad nickname. I kind of like it, actually."

"If my parents hear it they'll totally flip out. They think nicknames are low-class."

"Then you got yourself a mess of trouble, Hayseed," Luella said, closing her locker.

What Jeremiah did like about the nickname was that it wasn't about the color of his hair, or the fact that his family was rich. It was because of something he wanted to be. A banjo player.

After a few days people asked him when he was going to bring his banjo back to school. So he did, and at lunch time he played all the tunes he'd played before. He also played a new one, "Cripple Creek." It had a high, bouncy first part and then a lower part with some slides that sounded like long *waahs*.

He even screwed up his courage to sing "Little Birdy," although not very loud. Three or four people came to eat their lunch nearby. Some teachers stopped to listen. A couple of younger girls even hooked their arms together and laughed as they skipped in a circle.

It was strange how playing the banjo made Jeremiah feel different. He was no longer just a kid who didn't have many friends. He was the kid who could build a musical instrument and learn to play it.

He was a musician.

"I HOPE YOU'RE practicing enough," Jeremiah's mother said at dinner. "That Bach is pretty tricky. And I know how much you want to redeem yourself after the last talent night. Don't you, sweetie-pie?"

"Actually," Jeremiah said, pushing his shrimp creole around on his plate, "I was thinking maybe of not being in talent night this time. Just for a break."

"We understand," said his father. "We really do. It's just like your mother and me with some of our other inventions. Remember that combination toaster and peanut butter spreader that we invented? We thought it was going to be a big hit."

"And it would have been," said his mother. "If it weren't for the small issue of the electric shocks."

"Fortunately, no one got hurt."

"Well, there was that one incident…"

"*Singed* might be the word for it."

"Oh, yes, we were in despair," his mother said.

"And look at us now. You have to get back on that stage, Jeremiah."

Jeremiah didn't want to let his parents down, especially when he was feeling guilty for not telling them about the banjo. But Maestro Boris was less thrilled by Jeremiah playing Bach.

"I don't think the boy is up to it," he said, taking a gulp from the glass of fine French wine that Jeremiah's mother had just handed him. "One of my easier studies might be more suitable. Perhaps 'Pedagogical Study Number Two.'"

"Please, Maestro Boris. Jeremiah is very eager."

"If you insist."

"Do you hear, Jeremiah? You must be so excited."

No, Jeremiah thought. "Yes," Jeremiah said.

Jeremiah did not want to have another fiasco up on the stage of Fernwood Academy, so he practiced the piano until the keys swam before his eyes. And then for his own pleasure he went upstairs to his room and played the banjo. The notes that were so hard to find on the piano just appeared under his fingers on the banjo.

He didn't want his parents to hear, and his playing had become louder. So he devised a barrier to keep the sound from leaking beyond his door. He built a wall of pillows from floor to ceiling and another wall of his old stuffed animals, held in place by three pairs of skis leaning against them.

On the evening of talent night, Jeremiah had dinner with his parents. In the middle of the meal he turned so cold that his teeth actually chattered. Then he grew hot and felt that he might faint. He didn't want his parents to see, so he pretended to tie his shoelaces, keeping his head down and breathing slowly.

"I must say, this is a night your father and I have been looking forward to," said his mother. "The truth is, for a while there we thought we were pushing you too hard."

"Yes, all that time you've been spending in your room had us wondering."

"Wondering?" Jeremiah said, sitting up.

"Wondering why you needed all that rest."

Jeremiah blushed and took a sip of water from his crystal glass.

"I'd better get ready," he said.

In his room, Jeremiah put on a new shirt, a freshly ironed school tie, his blazer and gray pants and silk socks and polished shoes. When he went downstairs his parents were waiting, his mother in a shimmering evening gown and his father in a tuxedo.

"Come here, son," said his father. "We've got a little something for you."

"Really, that's not necessary."

"But we insist. Bring it here, will you, Monroe?"

The chauffeur appeared holding a bulky package. He put it on a side table and looked sympathetically at the younger Birnbaum.

Jeremiah undid the wrapping. Inside was a marble head on a stand. Long curls. Prominent nose and round cheeks. A scowl on its face.

"It's Johann Sebastian Bach himself," said his mother. "You can sit it right on the Hoosendorfer to inspire you."

"That's…really great," Jeremiah said. "Thanks a lot."

"Look at the time!" said his father, glancing at his watch. "We don't want to be late."

Monroe drove them to the Academy. There was a line of cars in the circular drive and they waited their turn to reach the front doors. Some of the students carried violin or trombone cases. Some wore dance costumes under their coats. Others carried sheet music under their arms.

Mr. and Mrs. Birnbaum walked with their son up the stairs, greeting other parents on their way to the auditorium.

There were still a few seats near the front. Jeremiah saw Luella come in with her parents. Her mother and father weren't dressed up like Jeremiah's parents. Luella herself wore a T-shirt with a skull on it above a frilly skirt, leggings and black boots.

She waved like mad when she saw Jeremiah.

He saw Maestro Boris enter, sniffing the air and raising one eyebrow. He saw Damien Mills nervously winding his tie around his fingers.

Soon the auditorium was packed. The lights dimmed, and a spotlight appeared on the stage. Principal Markworthy came out, tripped over a music stand, caught himself from falling, and smacked his chin against the microphone.

"Welcome progenitors, disciples and pedagogues," the principal intoned. "We have reached the breadth and compass of our school year and find ourselves at this crowning night. As you know, at Fernwood Academy we strive to produce students with manifold talents and accomplishments. Being able to brazenly present yourself before an audience is a valuable skill. And now, let the manifestation begin!"

"He's a fine speaker," whispered Jeremiah's father.

"Yes, a most impressive vocabulary," agreed his mother.

Principal Markworthy called out the name of each student in turn. One by one they came up and played the piano, the cello, the flute. Jeremiah could tell where each student's family sat in the audience, because the cheering from that spot was always the loudest.

Luella played a piece by Schubert on her violin. She liked what she was playing — Jeremiah could see that by the way she swayed to the music. It sounded good to him, too.

Damien Mills came up with the saxophone. He didn't play very well. In fact, at one point he sounded like a honking car. Jeremiah couldn't help feeling just a little bad for him. But Damien's friends whistled and hooted anyway.

At that moment Jeremiah wished that he had done something — hand out ten-dollar bills, maybe — to make more friends who would cheer for him.

Jeremiah waited for his name to be called, hoping all the while that somehow Principal Markworthy would forget him. But before long the principal skipped up to the microphone again, being careful not to hit his chin this time. Instead, he grabbed it and pulled it so close to his mouth that a feedback squeal made everyone cover their ears.

"Sorry about that," the principal said. "And now, Jeremiah Birnbaum."

As Jeremiah stood up, he felt his legs wobble. He walked slowly up the aisle and then up the steps to the stage. He sat down on the bench and stared at the piano keys.

He couldn't remember anything about playing the piano. He couldn't even remember which note the piece started on.

He felt beads of sweat on his forehead. He put out his hands but still he couldn't remember.

He gently touched a key. No, it wasn't that one. Nor that one, either.

A bead of sweat rolled down Jeremiah's forehead, along his nose, hovered a moment at the tip, and dropped onto a key. Maybe it was a sign, Jeremiah thought. He pressed the key.

But it wasn't that one, either. He stood up. He didn't know he was going to stand up. He just did. The lights shone down on him. He couldn't see any faces. Just a vast audience staring at him. He tried to say something, to apologize or excuse himself, but no words came out of his mouth.

And then he ran.

• • •

HE RAN to the edge of the stage and hopped down. He ran up the aisle, past his parents and all the other shocked faces. He heard exclamations of surprise, gasps and even laughter. But none of it made him slow down. He hit the door with both hands, making it swing open, and sprinted down the hall and out the front door.

Jeremiah didn't stop until he was under the maple tree. It was dark, with only some winking stars above. He slumped down to the ground, letting his back slide against the bark of the tree.

What had he just done? His parents were going to be humiliated. He'd made himself into the school freak.

At the same time he had to admit that he was glad to be off that stage and away from the piano. Jeremiah breathed in the cool air and felt the familiar ground under him. He heard a lone cricket chirping nearby. He looked up and saw a moving pinprick of light — a shooting star or distant airplane.

How was he going to make himself find his parents and go home?

In a minute, he told himself, closing his eyes. Or maybe two.

And then he heard a voice.

"Okay, so it wasn't your finest moment." It was Luella.

"It didn't take you long to find me," he said.

"Yeah, I'm a real genius. Or maybe it's because I sit with you here every day."

"As long as no one else finds me. Ever."

"Ever is a long time, Hayseed."

"You can call me Hayseed. You can call me Loser. Nothing could make me feel worse."

"Maybe. But I've got something that could make you feel better."

Jeremiah saw her pull something from behind her back. Even in the dark he could recognize the Flower Power gig bag. She held it out to him.

"How did you get that?" he asked.

"I asked Monroe to bring it. He put it in the trunk. He's a good guy, Monroe."

"I know he's a good guy. But why did you bring it? The concert must be over any minute."

"I didn't bring it for you to dazzle the Fernwood community. I brought it for you to play. For yourself. It always makes you feel better when you play, doesn't it?"

"I guess so."

"So, play something."

Jeremiah closed his eyes again, hoping as he once had as a little kid, that when he opened them everything would be different. But when he did open his eyes it was still dark. He was still sitting under the tree, and Luella was still holding out the Flower Power gig bag.

So he took it from her. He unzipped the bag and pulled out his banjo. He stuck it on his lap and tuned up. He sighed deeply. Then he began "Barlow Knife."

And as he picked and strummed, as the fingers of his left hand deftly found the notes in the dark, he felt a little better.

He picked up the tempo and added some double-thumbing to add melodic notes. Then he played "Salt River," and after that "Cluck Old Hen."

He stopped and took a deep breath of the night air. And then he heard another voice.

"How did you ever learn to play like that?"

It was his father.

Jeremiah looked up. Just beyond the overreaching branches of the tree he saw his parents standing and watching him. And near them were Luella and Monroe and Maestro Boris.

"Dad, Mom," he said, quickly putting down the banjo. "I'm sorry I ran out like that."

"Did you really build that yourself?" his mother asked. "Monroe said you did."

"The shop teacher helped."

"You know," his father said, "until now I've never actually heard someone play the banjo. It's a pretty nice sound."

"You really think so?"

"Absolutely."

Maestro Boris stepped forward.

"May I see your instrument?" he asked.

Jeremiah held it out and Maestro Boris

took it gingerly by the neck. He peered at it closely in the darkness, turning it upside down and around.

"A very interesting, if primitive, instrument. Of course many great composers were influenced by folk music. Beethoven. Dvorak. Real music always touches the soul. Even music from a...cookie tin."

He gave the banjo back to Jeremiah.

"Play another, Jeremiah," his mother said.

"I don't think — "

"Please," said his father. "For us."

Jeremiah sat down and began to play his latest tune, "Wildwood Flower." He didn't play it too quickly, but let the first low notes vibrate like someone twanging a fat elastic band. Then he let the bright, high notes of the second part ring out like tiny bells.

"Nice playing, Hayseed!" somebody called. Jeremiah saw Damien Mills passing by with his parents.

"Hayseed?" his father said. "Now *that's* going too far."

CARY FAGAN

10
Regular Life

JEREMIAH BIRNBAUM'S life did not dramatically change after talent night, but it did get a lot better. He still had homework, still had some of his after-school classes (although his parents let him drop etiquette), still took piano lessons with Maestro Boris.

He started to enjoy playing the piano a lot more, now that Maestro Boris allowed him to choose his own pieces. At school, kids quickly forgot about the spectacle of him dashing from the stage on talent night. When he played his banjo under the tree, some kids listened. Others ignored him.

But that was okay, Jeremiah thought. That was *normal*.

Banjo playing was just a regular part of life. It was a part of who he was and what he liked to do.

One day a new student, a girl with brown eyes and bangs, came up to him with a guitar covered in stickers. Her name was Marci Kalman.

"I know six chords," she said. "Want to jam?"

"Sure," Jeremiah said.

• • •

EARLY SUMMER meant warm weather, leaves on the trees and bright grass. It also meant another cross-country run.

As always, Luella slowed down her pace to keep Jeremiah company.

"I know what you're thinking," she said, as their feet pounded the gravel country road. They were well behind most of the other students.

"You always think you know what I'm thinking."

"Well, I do. You're thinking about that man."

Luella was right. Jeremiah had often thought about the man he had first seen playing the banjo, sitting on the porch of that abandoned farmhouse. He wished that he could meet him again and thank him.

"Seeing him the first time was a lucky fluke," Luella said. "It's not as if he's going to come back. Not even if he knew that he changed the life of Fernwood Academy's dorkiest student. You're not going to find him again."

"I know," Jeremiah said. "Let's take the short cut anyway. Just for old time's sake."

They headed for the old farmhouse. Luella chatted about how she was going to spraypaint her army boots gold, but Jeremiah wasn't listening. He was thinking about everything that had happened in the past year or so.

But then Luella stopped talking. Because she heard something. And so did Jeremiah.

Banjo playing. Playing that grew louder as they went around the corner of the house to the front porch.

The tune was "Roustabout." Jeremiah recognized it although he didn't know how to play it himself.

He and Luella looked at each other.

"We're going to be late getting back to school, aren't we?" Luella said.

But Jeremiah didn't answer. He was

already going up the porch steps, nodding to the man.

When the man saw Jeremiah, he nodded back and finished the tune.

"Well, hello again," he said. "So have you learned to play a little since we last saw each other?"

"Yes, sir," answered Jeremiah.

"I thought you might have." The man held out the banjo. "Show me, would you?"

So Jeremiah did.

A Note from the Author

MANY QUESTIONS remain unanswered about the history of the banjo, from its African origins to the modern instrument it has become. But one thing is sure. The early American banjos were handmade by individuals who wanted to play and a little later by woodworking craftsmen in small shops. And, yes, it is possible — and not all that difficult — to make your own banjo.

The wood for the first banjo that I made came from a broken Ikea chair. For the third and most recent one, I used wood that I found in the garage of our house (it looked like oak flooring). Two of the banjos have pots made from cookie tins. For one I used a hand-drum that looked something like a large tambourine. That banjo produced a better sound.

A search on the internet (using such words as "homemade banjo" and "cookie-tin banjo") will produce all kinds of photographs, drawings and plans. No two hand-crafted instruments are ever exactly alike, which is part of their charm. For the pot, people have used cigar boxes (an old tradition), gas cans, even wooden salad bowls with a skin stretched over the top. You can also see people playing homemade banjos on YouTube.

If you want to build your own banjo (or any other instrument), remember that tools can be dangerous. Always ask an adult for help. There are also books in the library and information on the internet about building simple homemade instruments out of cardboard boxes, plastic bottles, rubber tubing and the like. Building any instrument is fun, and making music by yourself or with others is a blast.

As for learning to play the banjo, there are plenty of instruction books and DVDs available, including some specifically for kids. You might even be able to find a real live teacher in your town. In *Banjo of Destiny* Jeremiah begins with a DVD called "Elements of Clawhammer Banjo." That's a real DVD starring Chris Coole, and it's a good one. Chris happens to live in my town, and is pretty much responsible for my own love of banjo. Thanks, Chris!

Some more thank yous are in order. To Shelley Tanaka and Patsy Aldana and Michael Solomon and Nan Froman and everyone else at Groundwood. To Rebecca, Sophie (Ms. Red Pencil herself) and Yoyo for first reading and commenting on the manuscript. And to all the amazing kids I've seen playing banjo (and mandolin and guitar and fiddle) at music festivals in the past few years. Some of the inspiration for Jeremiah came from them.